SOUP ON FIRE

Books by Robert Newton Peck

A DAY NO PIGS WOULD DIE
PATH OF HUNTERS
MILLIE'S BOY
SOUP
FAWN
WILD CAT
BEE TREE (POEMS)
SOUP AND ME
HAMILTON
HANG FOR TREASON
RABBITS AND REDCOATS
KING OF KAZOO (A MUSICAL)
TRIG
LAST SUNDAY
THE KING'S IRON
PATOOIE
SOUP FOR PRESIDENT
EAGLE FUR
TRIG SEES RED
BASKET CASE
HUB
MR. LITTLE
CLUNIE
SOUP'S DRUM
SECRETS OF SUCCESSFUL FICTION
TRIG GOES APE
SOUP ON WHEELS
JUSTICE LION
KIRK'S LAW
TRIG OR TREAT
BANJO
SOUP IN THE SADDLE
FICTION IS FOLKS
THE SEMINOLE SEED
SOUP'S GOAT
DUKES
SPANISH HOOF
JO SILVER
SOUP ON ICE
MY VERMONT
SOUP ON FIRE

SOUP
ON
FIRE

Robert
Newton Peck

Illustrated by Charles Robinson

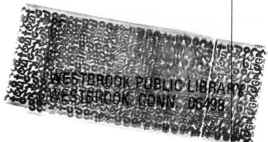

DELACORTE PRESS/NEW YORK

Published by
DELACORTE PRESS
1 Dag Hammarskjold Plaza
New York, New York 10017

Text copyright © 1987 by Robert Newton Peck

Illustrations copyright © 1987 by Charles Robinson

MANUFACTURED IN THE UNITED STATES OF AMERICA
9 8 7 6 5 4 3 2

Library of Congress Cataloging in Publication Data
Peck, Robert Newton.
Soup on fire.
Summary: Rob and Soup set in motion a wild scheme to catch
the eye of the Hollywood talent scout visiting their small Ver-
mont town.
[1. Vermont—Fiction.   2. Humorous stories]
I. Robinson, Charles, 1931–   ill.   II. Title.
PZ7.P339Soaam   1987   [Fic]   87-5261
ISBN 0-385-29580-4

SOUP ON FIRE

One

"Whoa," said Soup.

Pulling up short, I wheezed to a dead stop at Soup's house, in order to catch my breath. Then I walked to where Soup Vinson was lying in a hammock which sagged between two Vermont maple trees.

Soup grinned and wiggled his dirty toes. "Rob, let's have a race."

I panted. "Now?"

Soup was nodding and probable noticing that I was gasping for air, so that was the reason he offered so immediate a challenge. He was my best pal and closest neighbor. Soup's real name was Luther Wesley Vinson.

"How far?" I asked him.

"Oh," said Soup, "just to town."

"Into town?" I puffed, my bare feet kicking the dirt. "That's near to a mile distant. And I'm already winded from running all the way to here." I hauled in a breath. "How come you sudden want to run to town?"

"I found a nickel," Soup said, fishing it out of his pocket to flash in the early evening sunlight. "Soon as we locate ourselfs in town, we can end our race at the Gulf station and split an icy bottle of Orange Crush."

Seeing as I was hot and a mite dusty from running all the way from our farm to Soup's, a cold gulp of Orange Crush was more than any thirst could resist. And it could help me forget how smelly I was from evening barn chores.

"Rob, I'll even give you a head start."

"Okay," I agreed, considering my barren pockets, plus the grim financial reality that Soup owned a nickel and I didn't.

"On your mark," warned Soup, swinging his bare feet down from the hammock.

"Get set," I said.

"Go!"

We were off.

Taking an early lead, I peeked over my shoulder to Soup behind me, along the gravel road. He wasn't running at all. Soup was skipping. Maybe because he knew that we were running his first race of this Fri-

day evening, but my second, and he could easy over-
take me anytime he felt like doing it.

Soup was a year and four months older than I was,
and had sprouted longer legs.

Sure enough, just as I was legging it by the Method-
ist church, I heard Soup's rapidly gaining footsteps.
So I really turned it on. Nonetheless, he passed me
like I was parked. Well ahead, he sped around a bend
and out of sight.

By the time I finally made it all the way to the Gulf
station, Soup was already seated on the bright red
soda-pop cooler, smacking his lips and holding a totally empty bottle of Orange Crush.

You rat, I wanted to say. There wasn't enough wind
in my lungs to pump it out. Yet I wanted to deck him,
as sure as my name was Rob Peck.

After allowing me to fume for about a minute,
Soup smiled, then reached into his pants pocket and
produced his coin.

"It was somebody else's bottle," Soup admitted
with a wink, sacrificing his nickel to a slot in the
machine. "I wouldn't do that dirty to a pal."

Soup, however, didn't strain his generosity to offer
me the first swig. Or even the second. Inverting the
bottle, Soup gulped half of the Orange Crush and
then handed me the remains. I drained its energy-
packed carbonation (as the label claimed) in one
parched swallow.

Like many an early June evening, our Vermont

weather had really turned hot and muggy. My shirt felt damp with sweat. It was far from fragrant.

"We made it," I said, inserting a finger into the bottle's neck in order to lick off what I couldn't drink. "Right now, I don't guess I could run another ten feet." As I returned the empty bottle to a rack, the only air inside me resulted from Orange Crush bubbles.

Glancing down the street, Soup's freckled face suddenly twisted into a wide-eyed expression of alarm. Then he said the one word I didn't want to hear.

"Run."

Turning, I saw somebody coming our way. And it was no other than the toughest and meanest kid in school. Janice Riker! In less than a split second, Soup and I were galloping for our lives. I was praying that my recently consumed energy-packed beverage would refuel my tiring legs.

The energy part of the Orange Crush didn't seem to be offering any great help, but the carbonation was sure working. And it wasn't a leadpipe cinch to run while burping. Yet whenever Janice Riker was chasing me, which was usual no less than thirteen times a day, I managed to motor at an incredible speed. At such times, Soup called me Piston Peck, sometimes with slight variation.

I heard tell that whenever dogs race around a track, there's some kind of mechanical rabbit ahead of them, to spur the dogs to run faster. But here in our town of Learning, whenever kids run for their lives, there's no rabbit up ahead. Instead, old Janice is behind and closing.

"Soup," I panted, "I can't run another inch."

"Neither can I," he said, as the two of us sprinted around a corner by Jewel's Beauty Parlor.

"What'll we do?"

"Hide."

"But *where*?" I asked Soup as I peeked back around the building to see Janice storming our way on all cylinders. "Here she comes. And it looks like she's got a *rope*."

Being caught or cornered by Janice Riker was hardly a pleasure. In the past, as I was now clearly recalling, Janice had tied me to a spider-infested barn rafter, a beehive, and even to a log in Putt's Pond that was halfway submerged in muddy water. And her knots were usual tighter than a noon squint.

Some kids, like Janice Riker, are built for fighting. Soup and I were both about as chunky as a couple of broomsticks, and we were built for speed, not battle. On any given track, the two of us could outrun Janice on only one leg. But right now she was fresh and we were exhausted, a fact which tended to even the odds.

"Well," said Soup, "seeing as we don't have any place to hide, we've only two choices. Run, or fight Janice."

"Let's run," I decided quickly.

We ran.

Outrunning old Janice seemed a lot safer than attempting a suicide brawl. Janice Riker's fist was only slightly softer than a sledgehammer, and her muscles the size of a cantaloupe. I'd seen her bend a railroad spike and then dent it with her teeth. Her fangs had also dented *me* a few times.

"We gotta locate a place to hide, Soup," I said, hearing the last gaseous bubble of Orange Crush energy, as a result of hurried digestion, convert into furthering my forward propulsion.

The two of us stopped to look around.

Back behind Graziano's Grocery was an alley, yet we both knew it halted into a dead end. Across the street, however, was Mr. Jubert's Candy Store, the roof of which was low enough to offer refuge. All a kid had to do was climb up on the rain barrel and then execute a simple shinny to the roof.

We headed for Mr. Jubert's alley.

But the barrel was gone! How, I was wondering, could anyone be so uncaring as to remove a barrel in a town where Janice Riker stalked her victims?

Luckily for us, Soup and I had memorized a number of emergency escape routes, one of which was close-by handy.

Beyond Mr. Jubert's alley, a tall board fence stood as a barricade, yet one of its wider planks was loose, near the ground. Lifting it, Soup and I scooted through to the safety of its yonder side. Peering through a knothole in the fence, I saw Janice and her rope thundering our way at full throttle and prayed she wouldn't smell us. Janice had a nose like a blood-hound. Only larger.

She stopped, staring up at the roof of the candy store, and then sniffed.

"I know you guys are up there."

As I smiled, I figured that Janice had somehow forgotten about the missing barrel. I was hoping she'd also forget about *us*. But there's something about gulping down Orange Crush and its bubbles that always tickles my nose.

I sneezed!

Soup pulled his eye from another knothole.

"Oh, no. She heard ya, Rob."

"What'll we do?" I whispered.

Soup snapped his fingers. "I just thought of the perfect hiding place, somewhere that Janice wouldn't even think of looking."

"Where?"

Janice Riker was now pounding on the board fence, and it rattled like all fury. Louder than an empty wagon. Soup pointed over the top of Mr. Jubert's Candy Store, up at the sky. I looked, and there it was, a lofty haven of safety.

The big tall water tower.

Two

"You go first," said Soup.

I looked up. Rising almost straight into the air, the wooden ladder which rested tight against one of the four legs of the water tower seemed higher than I'd remembered. As I climbed, the ladder felt a bit loose.

Passing a sign which hung from a tower leg, I noticed the red letters.

DANGER

My bare foot tested the next rung.

"Hurry," said Soup, "before Janice sees us."

That did it. Rung after rickety rung, up the ladder I went, climbing higher and higher toward the big tank of water topping the tower. The tank itself was a gigantic container, in the shape of a rounded wash-tub, belted by several thick iron rings. Not even the rooster weather vane at the tip of our town hall stee-ple rose as high over the community of Learning as the water tank.

Clinging tightly to the ladder, I looked down.

"Keep going," Soup told me.

"We're almost above the clouds," I said. "Don't ya think we've already climbed high enough?"

"No," said Soup, "because unless we hide up inside the water tank, Janice could spot us up here for cer-tain. We'd be trapped."

I kept on climbing into the evening stratosphere, urged upward by the nagging fear that Janice Riker would see us. Looking down again, I saw her. She was far below, running along Main Street, looking into alleys and under the front porches of stores. A large dog bolted away from her in a droop-tailed panic.

It was hard to tell which one of us was shaking, me or the ladder.

As I made it to the top and slipped over the rim of the tank, Soup followed. Under the cone-shaped roof, it was darker. And warmer.

"Boy, am I hot," I told Soup. "And my clothes are starting to smell like a busy sewer. This shirt ought to get either burned or buried."

"Yeah," said Soup. "Mine too."

"I don't guess old Janice will ever dream that the two of us are up here."

In response, Soup crossed his fingers.

Inside the rim of the water tank ran a circular ramp, no more than a foot wide, all the way around. Upon this we lay panting. Just below us sat an enormous supply of water. The tank was fed by mountain streams and ponds, pumped upward and into the tank by a nearby windmill.

"Rob," said Soup, "I got a nifty idea."

I didn't answer. Because in the past, several of Luther Vinson's ideas had led only in one direction. Straight into mischief. Yet I was mutely curious.

"While we're up here," said Soup, "and waiting for Janice to give up and go home, maybe we could skin off our clothes and take a swim."

Eyeing the water, I had to admit that Soup's suggestion was more than tempting. All the running, not to mention a narrow escape from Janice, had near converted my body into a steam engine.

"Maybe," I said. "But it's only the first week of June. The water might be too cold."

Winters in Vermont, I knew, ranged from Thanksgiving to just about the middle of May, as our tons of snow melted at their own casual speed. June water, therefore, is only a few degrees warmer than liquid ice.

Soup yanked off his shirt.

"Rob, old sport, it'll be our first swim of the summer. On Monday, we can brag to all of the other kids how we braved it."

Inside, I was remembering what my mother had

repeatedly told me concerning the water tower. It was a place I was to keep clear of, and I'd heard Soup's mother echo a similar precaution. Yet here I was, high above every roof in town, removing my clothes. All I was wearing was a shirt and pants. No socks, no sneakers, and no underwear. As far as I was concerned, underwear was strictly for winter, and it was itchy enough then.

"Just think," Soup told me as he snaked out of his pants, "nobody's ever risked a swim up *here* before. We're pioneers! And maybe, if she hears about it, you'll impress Norma Jean Bissell."

As his argument strengthened, I took off my pants. A cooling dip, I was now reasoning, would sure feel great. Not to mention that Norma Jean might be awed by my daring.

"Okay," said Soup, "you jump in first."

I dunked a toe. "Wow! It's sort of . . . chilly."

"Good. It'll cool us off. Go ahead."

I went first. Soup followed.

To claim that the water was cooling us would hardly be accurate. More on target would be to admit that in one second we nearly froze. Soup's teeth were chattering like a nervous telegraph key.

So were mine.

We swam clear over to the other side, a diametric marathon of twenty feet, yet it seemed like we'd crossed Lake Champlain. Swimming back, I noticed a very odd object, one which seemed to be crawling on its legs along my trousers, which lay in a rumpled heap on the ramp. It appeared to be a very large spider. Or a crab.

As I swam closer, I could see that it wasn't a spider. Instead, it was a *hand,* one which picked up my pants and removed them. They disappeared over the rim. The hand returned, grabbing Soup's pants as well.

Then a face appeared.

"Ha, ha," said Janice Riker.

Soup and I looked at each other. Both of us, I figured, were aching to climb out of the icy water. But we sure couldn't do it while a *girl* was watching. I was feeling less like a swimmer and more like an iceberg.

"How's the water?" she asked. "Cold?"

"Beat . . . it . . ." Soup told her, shivering each word through purple lips.

"Naw," said Janice, "the view's too good from up here. I never watched nobody freeze to death naked. It oughta be fun."

As she waved our pants at us, I felt like a daisy with all of its petals pulled off.

I was praying that my burning dislike of Janice Riker would warm me a degree or two above zero. It didn't. In fact, it offered little more than a chilling effect. But then something happened. Somebody yelled. It wasn't Soup or Janice or me. Turning around, Janice looked to the ground, which was far beneath her. In panic, she dropped our trousers.

"Okay," she said to someone below, "I'll come down. But you oughta order them other two guys to climb down too."

As had our pants, Janice also disappeared.

Climbing out of the icy water, Soup and I peeked over the tank's rim and saw Janice Riker slowly inching her way down the rickety ladder. Below her, with his hands on his hips, stood our county sheriff, Dillon Blood.

"Oh, no," whispered Soup.

As we watched, we saw Janice finally reach the ground. She was talking to Sheriff Blood and pointing up our way. He had a grip on her hair.

"All right, you two boys," Sheriff Blood yelled to us in a voice that could have been heard in a sawmill, "come on down. Or the pair of you rascals will spend the night in jail."

Jail!

The word stabbed me like an icepick. It suddenly made me realize that I wasn't going to freeze to death. Instead I'd slowly die in prison.

Peering down from the rim of the water tank, I spotted a pair of pants. They were halfway down the ladder, caught on one of the rungs. The other pair of trousers lay below, on the ground, near where Sheriff Blood was now holding and scolding Janice.

"Soup, how are we going down the ladder without our pants? Janice is still there. She'll tell everybody in town."

"Right now!" shouted Sheriff Blood.

"If we go down," Soup said, "he'll grab us and haul us to jail."

As he said it, I could envision my mother's tear-stained face, looking through the bars at her only son. And I could hear Papa's voice telling me exactly what I'd get as soon as I got out. Yet here I was, high in the air, a kid from a good home who was no more than a frozen and naked criminal. My photograph would festoon our Post Office wall.

> CAPTURED
> Robert Peck
> NAKED TOWER CLIMBER

"If I have to climb up there and tote you young scoundrels down to ground," threatened Sheriff Blood, "you're going to be painful sorry."

I was already sorry. But now it was the *painful* part which was worrying me. And I certain knew the part of my body that might become painful. I was glad it was numb.

Buttoning his shirt, Soup said, "I'll go first."

His remark was a mystery. *Soup never went first.* I usual did. But there he was below me, climbing down the ladder. Down on the ground, Janice pointed up at Soup and laughed fit to bust.

I started down.

Below me, Soup had reached the one pair of pants that hung halfway down the ladder. "Good," he said, "these are mine."

Pulling them on, with difficulty, Soup continued his now-respectable descent and finally reached the ground. Wearing only my shirt, I followed, grateful that the evening was darkening, and that I was at least *backing* down the ladder. Even more thankful that my shirttail was extra long.

I made it.

Sheriff Dillon Blood was holding my trousers and wearing an icy expression. Soup grinned, Janice giggled, and I blushed. It sure was a relief when Sheriff Blood sent Janice home and tossed me my pants.

"Are we going to jail?" Soup asked him, as I was jumping into my jeans.

"You deserve to," he said, pointing at the DANGER sign. He touched one of the giant supports which held up the tower. "Boys, this here leg is real weak. The wood's rotten. Ought to get repaired, and sudden soon, before it buckles under the weight of all that water and the whole tower tumbles over and drowns the town. You lads could've got yourselfs killed." He shook his head. "Okay, hike on home. But before you go, I want you to promise me that you'll never climb that tower again."

"We promise," we both told Sheriff Blood.

He turned and walked away, as Soup and I headed straight as a beeline for home. We were almost there when Soup looked at me and grinned. "You won't believe this, Rob."

"Believe what?" I asked Soup.

He said, "I'm wearing your pants."

Three

The next day was Saturday.

But seeing as I'd been a mite tardy getting home last night, I didn't even bother to ask Papa if I could go fishing with Soup. Instead, I hustled some extra chores all morning long.

My pal, Luther Wesley Vinson, had shared with me his secret about getting-home time. Soup usual claimed, "It's best to arrive home too early for a spanking and too late for a bath."

It was actual Saturday afternoon that we were eagerly awaiting. Soup and I had agreed to go into town to the movies.

Soup arrived at noon, like usual, just in time to eat a

peanut butter sandwich with me. Our plan was to take in the double feature: Tex Ritter in *Rustler Guns,* followed by Fearless Ferguson in *Cliff Hanger.*

"Let's go, Rob," said Soup, his words sounding as if he was sinking into either peanut butter or quicksand.

In the kitchen, Aunt Carrie observed both of us with a suspecting eye. "Where are you rascals going?"

"Movies," I said.

"A double feature," Soup added.

"All picture shows do is ruin your eyesight," Aunt Carrie snorted. "Well, all I can say is, you both better be home well ahead of chore time. And not filthy dirty."

"We will," I promised her.

The two of us trudged our way to town, singing, throwing stones, punching each other, and generally inhaling all of the joyful bliss of a Saturday.

But we sure received one heck of a surprise when we finally arrived at State Theater, forfeited our dimes, and grabbed two seats in the very front row. The theater manager, Mr. Osgood Rivoli, stood up on the stage, raised his arms, and begged a hundred screaming kids for silence. Few of us obliged. Mr. Rivoli appeared not to be enjoying his job.

"Boys and girls," he said, over the continuing rumble of soprano chatter, stomping feet and squeaking seats, "there's a slight change in our program for today."

We responded with a murmur of distrust.

Mr. Rivoli continued. "Instead of Tex Ritter in *Rustler Guns,* we are proud to present a far better motion picture. We're showing the newest Hollywood child star and America's adorable sweetheart, Shirley Dimple, in . . . *Little Cutie Pie.*"

"It's a gyp!" yelled Soup.

"Boo!" I shouted.

We kids knew we'd been swindled. Nobody, not even Mr. Rivoli himself, ought to cheat a kid on Saturday.

Rising from our seats, we hurled popcorn boxes, candy wrappers and used gum (quickly torn from beneath seats) at a ducking Mr. Rivoli. Everybody hollered in protest. Fumbling for the slit between the curtains, he made a hurried exit from a storming barrage of rootbeer barrels, sneakers, baseball gloves, gumdrops, jawbreakers, bottlecaps, and half-eaten cones of melting ice cream.

"Rob, we ought to demand our money back," Soup said in a grumble.

"Right," I said. "But then I don't guess we'd get to see the second feature. I sure don't cotton to miss seeing Fearless Ferguson."

Soup agreed with a resigned sigh. "Yeah, missing Tex Ritter is sad enough."

The house lights dimmed.

For an almost eternal hour, Soup and I suffered watching Hollywood's child star and adorable sweetheart, Shirley Dimple, tapping and lisping her way into our overcandied indigestion. *Little Cutie Pie,* however, wasn't as bad as we feared. It was worse. Shirley tapped endlessly . . . along bowling alleys, boat docks and on the tops of pianos. When she didn't dance, she sang . . . to a kitten, a doll, a baby duck, a teddy bear and to assorted adult actors and actresses who were being paid to look enthralled.

"Maybe," said Soup, "at the end of this lousy movie, somebody will hit Cutie with a pie."

No such luck.

To make enduring *Little Cutie Pie* even more un-bearable, behind us sat two grownups, a man and a woman, who were oohing and aahing with Shirley Dimple's every tap and lisping lyric. They constantly whispered to each other, a conversation which I couldn't help but overhear.

"Isn't she adorable?" asked the woman.

"Yes," her husband replied, "but she's no cuter than our own little girl."

"You're right," the woman agreed. "Shirley Dimple isn't nearly as adorable as our little Janice."

Janice!

Even huddled in the safety of theatrical darkness, the name struck fear into my heart, a panic that could even overwhelm a hero such as Fearless Ferguson.

Turning around with caution, I recognized the pair of adults seated behind me. My guess had been correct. It was indeed Janice's mother and father,

Formica and Derel Riker. I recalled that Derel was Mr. Riker's nickname. His full name was Derelict.

Up on the screen, *Little Cutie Pie* finally lisped and tapped to a sugary fade-out as Shirley Dimple was rescued from kidnappers (a pity) and reunited once again with her kitten, duck, teddy bear, doll and a waving American flag.

"Thank gosh," sighed Soup.

Between features, as the projectionist was changing reels, Mr. Rivoli braved his second appearance on the stage. He was greeted by booing, razzing and one more bombing by confectionary litter.

"Boys and girls," he said, "before Fearless Ferguson comes on the screen, let me remind you to tell your mothers and fathers about our special, *adults only*, double feature next Saturday evening."

He waited for our hisses and catcalls to subside.

"Both of these films are starring the romantic duo of Hollywood, none other than . . . Miss Ardent Ample . . ."

"Oooohh," said Mr. Riker.

"And also Mr. Tungsten X. Kissel."

"Ah," said Mrs. Riker.

Mr. Rivoli continued his oral preview. "They'll be together again in both these pictures, *Tabasco Tootsie* and *French Giggles.*"

The Rikers mumbled their approval while Soup and I restated our loathing of love movies by making disgusting noises.

Once again, the theater darkened and our lives

brightened with one more perilous adventure of America's bravest hero, Fearless Ferguson. Holding our breaths, Soup and I sat wide-eyed with raptured reverence as Fearless overtook runaway wagons, untied helpless maidens from railroad tracks and scaled cliffs in order to rescue stranded lambs.

Gobs of unmasticated jellybeans remained tucked between my cheeks and gums, as I was far too entranced to chew. So there it all remained, inside my bulging face, creating its unmeasurable dental devastation. Even though I was ruining my teeth as well as my eyesight, I didn't honest care.

Before us, on the movie screen, no feat proved beyond Fearless Ferguson's coping.

Babies were snatched from burning buildings, and a canoe abrim with praying war veterans was kept from plunging to certain death over Niagara Falls. As dynamite fuses sputtered and hissed, shorter and shorter, Fearless somehow raced to the scene on time, by rail, leaping from the roof of one speeding boxcar to another as easily as hurdling a sidewalk crack.

"Wow," said Soup, as somebody's sweet old grandmother was retrieved from the dusty smoke of a caved-in mine shaft.

"Golly," I whispered, as an escaped man-eating tiger was roped and dragged snarling from a kindergarten.

Behind me, however, Mr. and Mrs. Riker seemed to be somewhat less entertained. It was, I learned from their conversation, *not* Fearless Ferguson whom they had come to see. Instead, they had somehow known it would be Shirley Dimple, in *Little Cutie Pie.* All during the Fearless Ferguson movie, *Cliff Hanger,* they constantly compared Shirley to their own delightful Janice, and Shirley Dimple was repeatedly evaluated as second best.

The final reel of *Cliff Hanger* blinked and flickered to its hair-raising end. Stepping over the mounds of trash which littered the aisle, Soup and I waited in the milling crowd of kids for our chance to exit.

After two hours in the dark, the late afternoon sunlight was almost blinding, and Soup and I squinted at each other.

"Rob," he said, as we were slowly walking toward home and chores, "do you reckon that we'll ever get to meet anybody famous in person?"

"No, I don't guess we ever will."

Little did I know.

Four

Sunday evening came.

Even though the threatening gloom of Monday morning and school hovered over us, Soup Vinson and I usual managed to enjoy every Sunday night for a very special reason. We Pecks didn't own a radio, but Soup's folks did, which meant only one thing.

From six-thirty until seven o'clock, the two of us were allowed to tune in to WGY and our very favorite radio program.

"The Green Maggot."

For exactly thirty thrill-packed minutes Soup and I huddled in the Vinson parlor, our ears glued to the fabric-covered amplifier of a humpbacked, fake-mahogany Emerson, sharing the daring of The Green Maggot, punctuated by static.

During the most exciting moments of gangster gunplay, the revolver shots sounded somewhat like small exploding paper bags. Yet we didn't care. The mobsters and jewel thieves were always shot, rounded up, and packed off to lifetime prison sentences. The dramatic conclusion was followed by spine-jolting organ music and The Green Maggot's deep-dungeon chortle: "You'll never know where The Green Maggot is tonight. He may be watching you. Ha, ha, ha, ha, ha . . ."

This particular Sunday evening's low-fidelity episode offered little variation from the usual finale. Virtue again triumphed over crime and The Green Maggot chuckled, reminding us that he'd be back again next week to face the challenge of his life, Dirty Doogan, the master criminal who had thus far eluded even *his* detection.

The Green Maggot was followed by a program which held minimal interest for either Soup or me. Not so for Soup's parents. What came next on radio station WGY was Mr. and Mrs. Vinson's favorite program.

"It's time," said an unseen announcer. Kettle drums rolled. "It's time for . . . Hollywood Heartburn's Talent Show!"

The studio audience went wild. Mr. and Mrs. Vinson, however, did not. They remained calm, perhaps due to decades of Vermont restraint, as though both of them descended from generations of fire hydrants. The faces of Soup's parents reminded me of a pair of nonticking clocks.

An orchestra blared the familiar theme song, then lowered its volcanic volume enough for the announcer to inform us that his radio program was . . . "sponsored by . . . Bathsheba Bubble Bath, the beautiful pink powder that smells of strawberry blossoms and bubbles your tub, your body, and . . . your love life!"

The music was echoing its approval of Bathsheba Bubble Bath, and so was the studio crowd.

"Are you feeling blue? If so," the announcer gushed, "stop in at your local drugstore, and treat yourself to a pinker life, that one irresistible pleasure that the most glamorous Hollywood stars enjoy, and one which every lady in America deserves . . . a luxurious soaking in a galaxy of floating pearls . . . Bathsheba Bubble Bath. It's strawberry-scented. And remember . . . Bathsheba soaks you every time."

Listening to the announcer talking about Bathsheba Bubble Bath, I was silently thinking, wasn't nearly as enjoyable as The Green Maggot. Yet, within me, the sales pitch was striking a responsive chord. At school, Norma Jean Bissell confided to me that she was currently bathing in Bathsheba's bubbles, and rewarded me with a brief, yet fragrant, whiff of its petalic residue.

Norma Jean had also hinted that if I smelled more

like pinky soap bubbles and less like our brown cows, my person would have more winning appeal.

Secretly, I was toying with the adventurous notion of giving Bathsheba Bubble Bath a try. Yet I knew better than to divulge such a sentiment to Soup. However, as my earlier attempts to awe Norma Jean had failed (including my gift to her of a slightly mashed red shoe box containing a toad) I concluded that perhaps a blossomy bathing might win me romantic rewards even beyond fantasy.

On the radio, a lady singer was warbling a song entitled "Sweet Violets," while I was fervently wishing that, instead of being Rob Peck, I was no other than Fearless Ferguson.

Now *that* would impress Norma Jean, and she would no doubt be prompted to bestow emotions equal to mine.

"Sweet Violets" ended.

The announcer added more testimony about Bathsheba Bubble Bath and the captivating effect its magic pink bubbles produced on the helpless victim, the object of one's heart.

"Stay tuned to the very end of tonight's radio presentation," the announcer cautioned, "because Mr. Hollywood Heartburn has a special surprise that you good people out in Radioland can't afford to miss."

Dutifully, we all stayed tuned.

"And now," said Hollywood Heartburn, "a very special talent act, and here he is . . . Mr. Lomax

Dickle . . . and his incredible impersonations of some celebrities you'll recognize and adore."

Mr. Dickle then imitated Mickey Mouse, President Roosevelt, Donald Duck, the Lone Ranger (including the galloping hoofbeats of Silver) and topped off his act by singing like Bing Crosby and cracking jokes like Fred Allen and Jack Benny.

"It sure is amazing," said Soup's mother, "the talent some people have these days."

"Sure is," said her husband.

For a capper, Mr. Dickle performed his impression of Shirley Dimple tap-dancing. Soup and I looked at each other with a shared revulsion.

When the hooting accolade for Mr. Lomax Dickle finally subsided, Hollywood Heartburn reminded us of how this evening would mark the last of his radio shows until fall. The studio audience moaned its regret.

"However," he said, "along with the sad news, there's some happy news to crack a grin on all your faces."

The Vinsons resisted smiling.

A trumpet fanfare almost blasted the Emerson radio into brass-encrusted fragments. Again, drums rolled. This, we knew, was *the big news*. The headliner.

"But first," said the announcer, "an important word about our sponsor's product."

We waited out this message.

"Bathsheba Bubble Bath now contains," the whispering announcer confided in us, "a fabulous new ingredient. Its name is . . . K-34."

"What's that?" Soup asked the radio.

"What is K-34?" the announcer quizzed us. "Well, it's a secret emollient that actually *emulsifies* as you bathe. K-34 deep-cleans your pores, and its purpose is to keep you bubble soft and kissing sweet."

I thought about Norma Jean Bissell, wondering if a mere single soaking in Bathsheba Bubble Bath would make me smell floral enough for her discriminating greenhouse taste. Would it convert me from cow to cowslips?

"Bathsheba Bubble Bath," the announcer continued to say, "now with miracle ingredient K-34, will make your entire life a romantic strawberry-scented encounter."

Ah, I mused, a romantic encounter with Norma Jean Bissell would be the answer to even my most exotic dreams. I wouldn't have to be Fearless Ferguson or Tex Ritter. All I had to be, to win Norma Jean's favors, would be Rob Peck and his irresistible emulsified pores . . . thanks to K-34.

"And now," announced the announcer, "the moment that all you loyal and faithful listeners out in Radioland have so patiently waited for."

Drumroll.

"Folks," said the voice of Hollywood Heartburn, "as I told you earlier, this is the final program of our spring season. But here's my surprise. Tomorrow, the Hollywood Heartburn Talent Show goes on the road.

We're going up into New England. And this week, we'll be scouting for movie talent. Not in big cities. We're going to small towns. Our first stop is a place that perhaps you've never heard of."

We all held our breath.

"The town is . . . Learning, Vermont."

Soup and I looked at each other in total disbelief. This was such a shocking delight that even Mr. and Mrs. Vinson reacted. "Well, I'll be," said Soup's mother. "They're all coming to *here*."

"Doggone," said his pa.

Other than this spirited outburst, the Vinsons continued to repress their raging enthusiasm, their Vermont faces remaining less animated than granite tombstones.

Hollywood Heartburn continued to explain how, even in tiny towns such as Learning, he could discover talent, and then offer Hollywood movie auditions. A chance for fame as well as fortune. Perhaps a trip to California for a screen test, plus an opportunity to meet famous actors and actresses. Even the stars, such as Ardent Ample and Tungsten X. Kissel.

"I won't be scouting for talent alone," Hollywood Heartburn said. "With me will be our entire Talent Hour crew . . . and . . . a special Hollywood guest star you moviegoers all know, by name and by reputation."

I couldn't breathe. Who, I was wondering, would be coming to Learning? What famous movie star could it be?

Another drumroll.

"This coming Saturday, in the tiny town of Learning, Vermont, . . . you'll be meeting nobody else but . . . Fearless Ferguson."

Sleep that night was impossible. Because in only six more days, I'd meet a movie hero.

In person.

Five

"Chile," said Miss Kelly.

Sitting at my seat behind a book, my attention strayed from the multicolored map in *Frontiers of Geography* in order to study more enticing topography, that of Norma Jean Bissell.

With every sly glance in her direction, my heart hastened with enrapt devotion. She was wearing a multicolored dress. In school, Norma Jean sat several rows away, almost a light-year, too far to allow my inhaling of even a subtle hint of her strawberry-scented Bathsheba Bubble Bath.

Up front, seated behind her desk, Miss Kelly again mentioned something about being *chilly*, even though it was June. Our final week of school. I stared blankly into my geography book, at the continent of Africa.

I wasn't being overly attentive.

Miss Kelly was talking about some other chilly place called the Andy's Mountain, and snow, without bothering to inform us exactly who Andy was. So I figured that he was a mountain climber, and Andy's Mountain was so high and so cold that Andy got chilly.

"And," our teacher continued, "when it's summer here in Vermont, it's winter in Chile."

To me, winter meant Christmas. And as I was sneaking another peak at Norma Jean, I half-heard Miss Kelly explain something about Santa Claus, only down on Andy's Mountain the chilly people called him Santiago.

This, I reasoned, would be useful information, because Miss Kelly would soon be giving us our final exams. Now I was prepared to show off all I'd learned about *their* Santa Claus, and how chilly he felt up on Andy's Mountain, because it surrounded the South Pole. I'd turn in a test paper that Miss Kelly would never forget.

As I stared at Africa, it seemed to me that *Frontiers of Geography* offered little help toward my locating the South Pole . . . or the person who probable lived there with Santiago. His aunt.

Her name was Aunt Arctica.

Miss Kelly was explaining some other stuff about

Santiago's aunt. She kept a pet. I don't guess it was a canary or a parrot. It was what our teacher called an Admiral bird. Maybe it was so chilly where Aunt Arctica lived that her bird had to perch on the South Pole. Even though I was looking at Norma Jean Bissell, I was still soaking up plenty of useful facts for my geography test.

Somebody knocked at our schoolhouse door. When our teacher opened it, I was surprised to see Mrs. Stetson come marching in.

I knew her rather well. Mostly by reputation. Mrs. Stetson, according to what people usual claimed, was our town's leading expert on religion, who knew the Scriptures backward and forward and could recite chapters and verses from memory. She did so at every opportunity. Rarely by request.

Mrs. Stetson's clothes were always black, and her face constantly seemed to glower with disapproval.

"He's coming!" trumpeted Mrs. Stetson, her lean index finger directed at the ceiling.

"She must mean Fearless Ferguson," whispered Soup, who was sitting on the bench beside me.

"Who's coming?" Miss Kelly asked.

Mrs. Stetson eyed our teacher with a stern glance of disbelief. "The most prestigious person ever to come to Learning. And he'll be here on Saturday for a religious revival that is sorely needed in this community. To give this town a *good cleansing.*"

"Somehow," said Soup, again whispering in my

ear, "I don't think she means Fearless Ferguson. It's somebody else."

Once again, Mrs. Stetson pointed directly upward, her face a study in grim determination and fervid devotion.

"Bishop Zion Zeal," she said. "And coming along with him will be his entire revival company, the Golden Prophets of Eternal Glory."

"You're right," I whispered to Soup. "She's not talking about Fearless Ferguson."

"No," he said, "she sure ain't."

"Well," said Miss Kelly, "this certainly is news."

Mrs. Stetson raised both her hands, all fingers extended. "News? I should say it's news. *Blessed* news! An opportunity for every child in this town to spend an entire Saturday on his knees. In prayer."

Soup softly groaned.

So did I. Even though I prayed prior to bedtime (and before arithmetic exams), an entire day on my knees didn't quite fit my plans for Saturday, especially when Fearless Ferguson and Hollywood Heartburn were arriving. It worried me. A situation like this could divide our town.

"That's not all," Mrs. Stetson continued in an inspired voice that seemed to be floating down from on high, someplace like Andy's Mountain. "Bishop Zion Zeal is also bringing us his host of gifted singers, the Golden Prophet Choir."

Miss Kelly looked surprised. "Really?"

"Truly be," said Mrs. Stetson. "And on every street

corner, their voices will be ringing out the anthem which was personally composed by Bishop Zeal himself . . . 'Rescued from the Burning Flames.' "

Without even a pause for breath, Mrs. Stetson began to sing. Her voice could only be described as something between a rusty chainsaw and a motorcycle kick-start. She must have been up all night gargling gravel. Each unsteady phrase scraped along my spine like a dull putty knife, until Mrs. Stetson attempted to hit a soprano note, one that really burned and flamed.

It would have turned The Green Maggot blue.

No pitch, regardless of how high, lay beyond her, as Mrs. Stetson gear-stripped her vocal cords with all the lilt of a lugwrench.

I had to credit Mrs. Stetson with her courage. Undaunted by her upper-registry failures, she attacked the final measures with a divinely inspired gusto that might have awakened the Egyptian dead.

I saw Miss Kelly wince.

At last, "Rescued from the Burning Flames" mercifully screeched to a stop like a deflating truck tire.

"Thank gosh," I heard Soup say, warily uncovering his ears.

"There are three more verses," explained Mrs. Stetson, "but I apologize for not having memorized the words."

"Oh," said Miss Kelly, "that's quite all right. But I'm sure the children enjoyed your singing."

Mrs. Stetson stiffened her spine. "I sing in the church choir, you know. Every single Sunday."

"Yes," said Miss Kelly, "so I've heard, even though I live across town."

"Rob," said Soup, "I always used to like music a lot. Up until today."

"Yeah," I said. "Me too."

"So," said Mrs. Stetson, "I just thought it best that I drop in here at your school, to inform the youngsters of their spiritual duties on this coming Saturday." She nodded. "A good cleansing."

"Thank you," Miss Kelly said. "That was extremely thoughtful of you, and we *all* appreciate your giving us the exciting news." She turned to face us. "Don't we, class?"

"Yes'm," we moaned.

"At home," Soup told me, "we got a grindstone wheel that can sing sweeter than that. A lot of her sharps were flats."

I giggled.

Miss Kelly shot the two of us a warning look as she was guiding Mrs. Stetson in the general direction of the door.

"Perhaps," said Mrs. Stetson, "you could teach the anthem I just sang to your students, so they'll be prepared to greet Bishop Zion Zeal by singing 'Rescued from the Burning Flames.'"

I saw Miss Kelly fake a nod.

"Well," she said, "that's a possibility."

As she exited, Mrs. Stetson squeezed off her part-

ing shot. "It's certainly about time our village considered being Rescued from sin's scorching furnace."

Mrs. Stetson left, and I saw Miss Kelly slump into
her desk chair, reaching for her bottle of Anacin. But
then our teacher slowly began to smile.

"Thank goodness," she said, "we have a fire department."

Six

School ended for the day.

Soup and I were, more or less, heading in the direction of home. But then my pal spotted something which had caught his eye. He pointed.

"Rob," he said, "there seems to be a crowd of people gathering around Miss Crump's house."

Miss Irma Crump, I knew, earned her meager living by giving music and dancing lessons. As we approached her house, I read the shabby sign which hung from a post on her front lawn:

```
┌─────────────────────────────────┐
│          Miss Irma Crump          │
│          LESSONS IN               │
│   ACTING, VOICE, AND DANCE.       │
│      ALL INSTRUMENTS.             │
└─────────────────────────────────┘
```

Usually there was nobody outside Miss Crump's studio. Once in a while, a hopeful mother could be seen dragging a small reluctant violinist, or some other resisting vocalist, or ballerina, toward the front door.

Today, however, was quite the opposite, and Miss Crump's business was booming.

Edging closer, I estimated that at least a dozen mothers stood impatiently in line, each matron firmly grasping the wrist of her squirming, escape-minded offspring.

The sullen captives were holding an arsenal of tarnished instrumental weaponry with which they would eventually assault and challenge the instructive capabilities of Miss Crump. Most of the musical instruments I saw appeared to have been recently resurrected from attic trunks, or garages, where they had remained unplayed for decades.

Several of the kids I knew by name.

Elmo Mazurski held a cornet. Cleo Finn had a cello. Mrs. Vinella was holding an accordion with one hand and her son, Albert, who was kicking and screaming, with the other. Hiding behind a tuba, which was twice her size, stood Mary Agnes Brocking.

Not all who waited for Miss Crump's instruction were children and mothers.

Mr. Stilson Leak, a local plumber, stood in line with a slide trombone. And a zither. A long-handled sink plunger hung from his belt. His wife, Helen, clutched a very large drum.

"Just think," I overheard Mrs. Leak tell her husband, "a week from today we could both be famous."

The plumber flushed with excitement.

Others were coming. Everyone seemed to be talking at once as they waited along Miss Irma Crump's front walk. There was, however, only one topic of conversation.

"I'm probable a mite rusty," explained Mr. Harvey Cleveland, fingering a French horn. "But years ago I played three seasons in the high school band."

The elderly woman beside him, Miss Thurman, muttered no answer, as she was busily occupied in blowing through a harmonica which was wired to her head, while also juggling three spangled Indian clubs. One of her clubs flipped higher than expected. It then fell, spinning crazily, landing with a *boom* on Mrs. Leak's drum.

The plumber's wife spoke a word which, I was concluding, wasn't intended to be complimentary. Grabbing her husband's sink plunger, she whacked Miss Thurman in the harmonica.

"There's going to be a fight," Soup said.

Soup was wrong.

Cooler heads prevailed. Mrs. Brocking and Mrs.

Mazurski managed to restrain Miss Thurman and Mrs. Leak from clawing each other apart. Gradually their tempers subsided and relative order was restored.

"Rob, old sport," Soup said, "I don't know how to tap-dance, and my singing really isn't anything to brag about."

"Me too," I told him. "And neither one of us own or play a musical instrument."

Soup leaned on a fence post. Looking at my pal, I could tell at a glance that Luther Wesley Vinson's mind was working. Soup had slipped into deep thought.

"What are you thinking about, Soup?"

"Well," he said, "seeing as Hollywood Heartburn is coming here to Learning, this Saturday, it'd be a downright shame if you and I didn't enter the talent contest."

"Yup, it certain would," I agreed.

"And there's only one thing holding us back, Rob."

"What's that?"

Soup sighed. "Between the two of us, we don't have a speck of talent."

"No," I said, "I don't guess we do."

Soup studied the line of people, kids and musical instruments which now awaited to threaten the professional guidance of Miss Irma Crump.

"We need some sort of a plan."

"No!" I said quickly.

In the past, whenever Soup Vinson figured out a

plan, it had always plopped the two of us into a pot of boiling trouble. Looking up, I saw the town water tower and its tank hovering above, and I remembered our unfortunate brush with Sheriff Dillon Blood. For a second or two, I could envision myself in jail, behind bars for life . . . and with Soup for a cellmate.

"How," asked Soup as he paced back and forth, "will we attract the attention of Hollywood Heartburn?"

"No," I said again, "no plan." As I spoke, my brain impulsively began to recap Soup Vinson's insane schemes, all of which had accomplished little except to goad us along the path to ultimate disaster.

Soup grinned. "Rob, I just happened to notice what you were doing in school today, during the geography lesson."

My spine straightened. "I was paying attention," I lied, "to what Miss Kelly was teaching us about Aunt Arctica."

Soup shook his head. "Not quite. You were paying more attention to the latitude and longitude of Norma Jean Bissell."

He was right and I knew it. There was, I secretly admitted, something special about Norma Jean that made her far more compelling than Argentina or all the rest of Africa.

"Just think," Soup told me. "Try to picture our winning the upcoming talent exhibition, and how

Norma Jean would practically throw herself around your unwashed neck."

Somehow, I pictured it.

The local crowd was cheering. Hollywood Heartburn was smiling. Mrs. Stetson wasn't singing. The whole town of Learning was chanting my heroic name. Rob Peck! Rob Peck! Rob Peck! And Norma Jean Bissell was stepping forward to reward me with momentary trophies, not to mention future adoration. In private. The vision was more than my perishable heart could resist.

"Okay, what'll we do?" I asked Soup.

He snapped his fingers. "I got it."

"It couldn't be singing, dancing, or playing some crazy musical instrument," I asked him, "could it?"

Soup's grin began to broaden from mild inspiration into total confidence. "No," he said softly, "not quite. Rob, you'll have to trust me. Because, this time, I may have managed to come up with a caper that could propel us both to stardom."

Like an idiot, I was on the verge of asking Soup what his idea would entail. My hands were starting to sweat. Had I any sense at all, I told myself, I wouldn't play any part in it. In my mind, I could still remember our narrow escape from Sheriff Blood. Yet curiosity bested reason, and I was itching to ask Soup for details.

Something disrupted my thinking.

"Rob," said Soup, "look who's coming."

I looked.

But it was difficult to believe what I saw. Along came Mr. and Mrs. Riker with Janice in tow. She wasn't the Janice we knew. Instead, she was dressed up as Shirley Dimple.

I heard Janice say a cussword.

"Come along, dear," Mrs. Riker told Janice. "It's your golden chance to become a Hollywood movie star."

On Janice's head was a blond wig. She wore a frilly dress. On her chunky legs, long white stockings. As far as I could notice, Janice didn't really look anything like Little Cutie Pie. She actually looked more like an extralarge marshmallow pizza.

Mouth open, I watched Formica and Derelict Riker bulling their way to the very front of the line, hauling their kicking daughter.

Pointing at her, I laughed.

Hearing my laughter, Janice shook a fist at me and promptly vowed what she'd do to Soup and me at school tomorrow. "I'm going to put your lights out," she snarled.

As she spoke, I felt lumps and bruises beginning to swell on my flesh.

"Ah," said Soup, "this only serves to bolster my plan." He turned to face me. "Rob, the entire town is going to try to impress Hollywood Heartburn. That makes our inventive artistry far more clever."

At that moment, I was considering that Soup was about to tell me how I'd glean the attentions of Norma Jean Bissell. Yet I was mistaken. Because good old Soup really surprised the living heck out of me. He was smiling as he announced the target of his scheme.

"We," said Soup, "will impress Fearless Ferguson."

"How," I asked, "are we going to do that?"

"Doing," said Soup, "what he wouldn't dare to do."

Seven

The week dragged.

To me, Saturday would never arrive and existed sometime in the next century. It would be a big day in my life, because maybe I'd get noticed by Norma Jean Bissell.

Another problem plagued my thoughts.

On Saturday, *two* groups of visitors were coming. Hollywood Heartburn's troupe of talent scouts *and* Bishop Zion Zeal and his Golden Prophets of Eternal Glory. Good people lived in Learning, yet this could start a *war.*

Soup had offered no particulars of his plan. At school, however, I'd observed that he had unfolded a large scrap of paper, studied it, and then quickly had returned it to his pocket. It seemed to be some kind of a map.

"What's that paper in your pocket?" I had asked him.

Soup had grinned. "Oh it's nothing at all, Rob. Just a rough idea of something that's cooking in my mind."

"Show it to me."

"Well," Soup had said with a shrug, "it's really not quite ready yet. But you'll be in on the deal."

Now, as the two of us were climbing Dugan's Hill, walking home from school, Soup stopped in the middle of the dirt road. Turning his head, he looked uphill at a place which was well known to both of us and to everyone else in Learning.

It was Wilbur's Wagon Repair.

Mr. Wilbur Wynfield's business establishment could hardly be called the most tidy place in town. Strewn about lay Wilbur's endless collection of wheels, spokes, rims, wagon tongues and tailgates . . . plus piles of loose boards of every length and width. All this, plus assorted junk and wire entanglements.

Nevertheless, most everyone in Learning gave Wilbur due credit. No matter what kind of a wagon a farmer owned, in need of repair, Wilbur Wynfield could supply the missing part.

"Rob," said Soup, "let's go look."

Mr. Wynfield didn't seem to be around. So Soup

and I strolled among the mounds of junk which were heaped here and there, much of it behind the repair shop.

I sighed.

"Junk collecting," I told Soup, "isn't exactly what's going to win a talent show."

"No," said Soup, "I don't guess it would." As he spoke, Soup moved a wheel to see what lay beneath it.

"Lots of other people can sing and dance or play some kind of a musical instrument," I said. "How are we going to play a song on a wagon wheel?"

"Talent," said Soup, as he tugged on a board, "isn't always musical. Sometimes, a talent act is *action.*"

I scratched my head. "Action?"

As he turned to face me, Soup was smiling. "I'll have to thank Mrs. Stetson," he said, "for giving me the whole idea."

"Mrs. Stetson?"

Soup nodded. "Yes, that remarkable lady who visited our school last Monday to warble her inspirational anthem."

I flinched. "You can't mean you enjoyed listening to Mrs. Stetson's 'Rescued from the Burning Flames.' "

"Sometimes," said Soup, as he resumed his pawing through the pile of junk, "it isn't the singing that's important. Instead, it's the *message* of the song. Mrs. Stetson won't know, until Saturday, how her anthem started an idea rolling in my brain."

"And," I said, "you're planning to pray when Saturday rolls around. We're going to pray on a wagon wheel?"

"Well," said Soup, "if we can pull it off, a prayer just might help . . . especially near the water tower."

Nothing that Soup was saying made any sense. But then, his explanations rarely did. As far as I could figure, Soup and Mrs. Stetson were going to pray with a wagon wheel underneath the water tower.

I pointed a finger at my friend.

"Soup," I said, "I'm *not* going near the water tower. I can still hear Sheriff Blood's warning that he'll throw us both in jail. And I'm certain not going to lose my pants again. Just think what Mrs. Stetson would have reported to our mothers if she'd seen our bare behinds."

Soup straightened up. "You win," he said softly. "We won't take our pants off at all. Not for Mrs. Stetson, or even for Bishop Zion Zeal."

I sighed with relief.

Yet I still was wondering about what Soup Vinson was planning to do. Rescue a wagon wheel? Or maybe rescue Mrs. Stetson. This, I was thinking, could be a pitfall. Mrs. Stetson knew Mama and Aunt Carrie, and ever since I could remember, she stopped by our place and ratted to them about my deportment.

Or lack of it.

Mrs. Stetson, I had long ago decided, was someone thoroughly to avoid. Come the weekend, I was aching to catch Norma Jean Bissell's eye. But certainly not the disapproving glances of Mrs. Stetson.

Soup's face appeared thoughtful. "Rob," he said, "you may not believe this, but what talent we have, we owe it all to Mrs. Stetson's song."

"I don't like it," I said.

"Trust me," said Soup. "Mrs. Stetson may have a singing voice like a hacksaw, but 'Rescued from the Burning Flames' has ignited a spark of genius." He tapped the tip of a finger to his head.

Soup, I had to admit, was a showman. Of sorts. On numerous occasions, his schemes had captured the attention of many a bystander. They had also landed us into trial and trouble. Thinking about jail and Sheriff Dillon Blood, I wasn't enthusiastic. Yet I was curious.

My curiosity heightened as I saw Soup sit down on an old wagon frame and remove the mysterious paper from his pocket. Inching closer, I squinted over his shoulder.

"It's a map," Soup explained.

"Of what?" I asked him.

"A map of our town." His finger touched a corner of the paper. "Here's where we are now, at Wilbur's Wagon Repair. And here's the center of the village."

"What's that round thing?"

"Oh," said Soup, "that's the water tower, which stands almost at the foot of Dugan's Hill, and that's here."

It was only a map, I told myself, and a map couldn't

get us into mischief. Or could it? The palms of my hands began to sweat. I was wondering if map-making could be considered a talent, like singing or playing the cornet. Knowing good old Soup as I did, I figured that he'd consider drawing a map too tame a hobby. One which wouldn't court somebody famous . . . like Fearless Ferguson.

"Soup," I said, "your map's okay. But it really isn't talented enough to get ourselfs into a Hollywood movie. Is it?"

"You'll see."

The way he said it made me feel a whole bit less fearless than Ferguson.

"Dugan's Hill," said Soup, "is what's going to put *us* on a map."

"A hill?"

"Not exactly the hill itself. The talent is what we *do* with Dugan's Hill, on Saturday. A hill means one thing, Rob. It means gravity."

I took a deep breath. "Soup, tell me that gravity doesn't have anything to do with Mrs. Stetson. She knows my mother, and I don't guess I want her to know *me.*"

"Don't worry," Soup told me. "We'll be almost out of sight during the entire performance."

"What are we performing?"

Soup grinned. "Mrs. Stetson's song."

" 'Rescued from the Burning Flames'?"

"Now believe me," said Soup, "if there's one caper

that will ignite Norma Jean Bissell, it's something that'll practically set her heart on fire."

"But we'll be out of sight."

"Uh, for a while. Our noble purpose is not one of hostility. In fact, quite the opposite. We're going to unite hostile forces. We'll be a link between the Golden Prophets of Eternal Glory *and* Mr. Hollywood Heartburn's Talent Show. Robert, you and I shall be heroes, and then modestly accept the laurels of the crowd. Not to mention clinching our chance to be in a motion picture."

"As movie actors?" I asked Soup.

"No," he said, "as stuntmen."

Eight

"Rob!"

I was asleep. In my dream, I was the bravest fireman in town, climbing a ladder and rescuing Norma Jean Bissell from two dangerous criminals.

"Rob, wake up."

Again I heard my name, but didn't want to awaken and spoil such a romantic dream. Up the rickety ladder I charged. Above me was the water tank, where Norma Jean was being held captive by Sheriff Dillon Blood and Mrs. Stetson. But as I heard my name in the night, I wasn't Rob Peck.

I was . . . The Green Maggot.

"Put on your pants," said Mrs. Stetson. "All of your

ugly green skin is showing. What you need is a good *cleansing.*"

Reaching the summit of the ladder, I yanked one of Norma Jean's pigtails, to free her, while Sheriff Blood swung at me with his billy club. Mrs. Stetson hit me with a strawberry-scented hymnal.

"Rob! It's me."

Ignoring the call, I leaned forward to receive my reward, a kiss from Norma Jean. But we were interrupted by Mrs. Stetson, who was singing a duet with Sheriff Blood.

"What's your prisoner number?" Sheriff Blood asked me.

I told him it was K-34.

"Rob. I'm outside."

I woke up. Leaving my bed, I stumbled to the open bedroom window to look outside and saw Soup. He was wearing his shirt and jeans.

"Put on your pants," he said.

"Why?"

"Because we gotta relocate the hay."

"What hay?"

"The hay we're going to use for our stunt on Saturday. So hurry up."

"Hush," I hissed. "If you wake up my folks, we'll both be sorry."

Soup quickly covered his mouth.

As I stepped into my pants, I was wondering why Soup and I were haying in the middle of the night.

Out of my window I crept, along the slanted roof and then down the apple tree.

"Let's go," said Soup.

We went.

While trotting across our meadow I wanted to ask Soup where the hay was stacked. Since we both lived on a farm, I figured it would be close by, but I was dead wrong. Before I knew it, we were approaching town.

"Where's the hay?"

"We're coming to it."

Soup pointed to a stack of last summer's hay that winter had nearly flattened to a pitcher's mound.

"No," I said. "That hay belongs to the Rikers. It's Janice's. She feeds it to her goat."

"Quiet," said Soup, as we approached the scattered hay, "or you'll wake up Janice, and she'll be out here and fixing to beat us up."

I stopped. "I'm not going to steal anybody's hay, Soup. Not even Janice's."

Hands on his hips, my pal looked at me with lessening patience. "Nobody said anything about *stealing*. We're only going to *borrow* an armful or two. Janice will never miss it."

"Her goat might," I said. "I've seen that goat of hers, and he's almost meaner than Janice. The only difference is that the goat smells better."

"Weren't you in school today?" Soup asked.

"Sure I was."

"Well, didn't you overhear Janice complaining to

Miss Kelly that her parents sold her goat to pay for the tap-dance lessons at Miss Crump's?"

"No," I said.

Soup waved both arms. "So you see," he said with a grin, "this hay's only going to waste . . . unless we use it."

"Okay," I said, too sleepy to argue.

"Pick an armful," Soup said, "and we'll get started."

Bending, I hefted up an armful, feeling the hay itching my naked chest. Soup picked up a bit less of a load than mine.

"Where to?" I asked Soup.

"Just follow me, old sport."

"But where are we toting this hay?"

"Not very distant. We only have to cart it as far as the top of Dugan's Hill."

As I followed Soup, I began to wonder about Dugan's Hill and why we had to take hay there. I sighed. There was scant reason in so many things that Soup devised for a midnight romp.

"We have to hide it," Soup announced as he stopped at the crest of Dugan's Hill. Below us, the lights of Learning were long extinguished, as all the good citizens of town were in bed . . . where I was wishing to be.

"We're hiding it?" I asked.

"Of course," Soup told me. "We can't risk the chance of somebody else's taking it." He chuckled. "If there's anyone I can't stand, it's a hay thief."

Soup looked around.

So did I. "Okay," I said, "where do we hide it?"

"Over there."

In a daze, I followed Soup in the dark, carrying my hay as he also carried his, again wondering where he was going. I should have guessed. The answer almost jumped up and slapped me in the face. Suddenly, we were there, standing behind Mr. Wilbur Wynfield's Wagon Repair place.

"Let's bury it," Soup said.

Too tired to argue, I helped Soup create a hole in the rubbish large enough to hold our hay.

"It's not enough," said Soup.

We returned to Janice Riker's for several more loads. I couldn't reason why we needed the hay, and I was too worn out to ask Soup. Long ago, I'd decided that midnight was no time to cross-examine the insane. Maybe my pal was hoping to stuff Mrs. Stetson.

Depositing our last armfuls of hay into our cavity, Soup and I dragged an old tarp over the hole, to mask our stash.

"That does it," said Soup.

"Thank gosh," I said. "We both ought to get a good night's sleep, because you know what tomorrow is."

Soup nodded. "It's our geography test."

Walking home, I confessed to Soup that I really wasn't cocksure of all my facts about Africa, especially in troubling areas like Argentina, and the chilly place, Andy's Mountain. But he convinced me that my command of Santiago and his Aunt Arctica would surely amaze Miss Kelly, considering my vast knowledge of the Admiral bird which perched on the South Pole.

Soup giggled. "Rob, old sport, I bet nobody in all Vermont knows what you do about Africa."

I don't know what time it was when I finally crawled back into bed. I didn't even bother to take my pants off, because sun-up chores would probable be coming due at any moment.

Closing my eyes, I tried to resume the romantic dream about my heroic rescue of Norma Jean Bissell, hoping that it would be somewhere in a soft mound of hay. No such luck. Instead of kissing Norma Jean, my snoring lips were now pressed to another face.

Janice Riker's goat.

Nine

It was Thursday.

As it turned out, the geography test Miss Kelly gave us wasn't as hard as I had expected. It was harder. And trickier, because there was a drawing question which hinted that Santiago was somewhere in South America.

Not remembering too clearly what Santiago looked like, I drew a picture of Aunt Arctica. It included Admiral, her bird.

I felt greatly relieved when the school day ended, and Miss Kelly released us from the shackles of learning.

Soup and I headed uproad.

To relieve the boredom of a long hike, Soup and I often walked home from school by taking a different route. Today was no exception. The two of us were strolling along Main Street when a certain somebody caught my eye.

"Look," I said, "there's Mrs. Stetson."

She wasn't alone. Several other ladies were with her, and all of them were wearing black dresses.

"They're carrying signs," Soup said. "On sticks."

At first, I thought the women were merely *walking* along on Main Street, as other shoppers were doing. But no, Mrs. Stetson and her companions seemed to be *marching*, knees high, in single file. Mrs. Stetson was in the lead, her sign pumping up and down with the disciplined rhythm of a majorette's baton.

Soup and I stopped to watch.

"Something's up," Soup told me, "other than her sign."

The ladies in black, hoisting their signs aloft, paraded by the State Theater. Then, pivoting into an abrupt about-face, they reversed their direction to march past the picture-show theater again. They repeated their maneuver over and over in a close-order drill that might have surpassed the precision of West Point cadets.

"Let's go see," said Soup.

Edging closer, yet hidden behind a wagon loaded with sacks of sorghum grain, we could read the letters which were printed on Mrs. Stetson's sign:

SATAN GOES
TO PICTURE SHOWS.

Another sign read as follows:

*The Prophets
are coming.*

A third sign asked . . .

HAVE YOU BEEN
RESCUED?

These signs, however, were not the only signs we saw. Plastered against the outside of State Theater, to the left and right of the box office where the movie tickets were sold, were two large full-color posters. These were advertising the pair of adults-only movies which were scheduled as the double feature for Saturday evening.

Having seen the posters earlier that week, I recognized the famous faces and their names. It was Hollywood's romantic duo, Miss Ardent Ample and Mr. Tungsten X. Kissel. *Tabasco Tootsie,* one poster read. The other . . . *French Giggles.*

If there was one brand of movie that Soup and I avoided, it was a *love* picture. I wasn't at all interested in spending a dime to watch Mr. Kissel smooching Miss Ample.

Mature patrons, perhaps, felt more enthusiasm.

As we watched, a gentleman stopped to study the *French Giggles* poster and seemed more than mildly captivated by the lipsticked face (not to mention the satiny lace nightie) of Miss Ardent Ample.

Up behind him crept Mrs. Stetson.

Closing in on his undefended ear, she honked her message. "Satan goes to picture shows!"

The man fled.

"Fear not, brother," hollered Mrs. Stetson as she waved her sign. "Bishop Zion Zeal is en route. The Golden Prophets of Eternal Glory will be coming, and you'll be *Rescued!*"

"Let's get out of here," I told Soup, fearing that Mrs. Stetson would discover us and try to *Rescue us* right there on Main Street.

"Not yet, Rob," said Soup.

"Why not?" I whispered.

"Because," he said, "here comes another victim. Maybe we can watch Mrs. Stetson and the other ladies do some *Rescuing.* I never saw anybody Rescued before. Maybe she'll do it like Fearless Ferguson."

"Maybe," I said, preparing to bolt.

Turning about, Mrs. Stetson spotted her prey, as the man had paused to admire Miss Ample's assets, which were ripely displayed. He was smiling at the *Tabasco Tootsie* poster.

Stalking him as a cat after a mouse, Mrs. Stetson closed in on tiptoe. She then roared her opening salvo, causing the unsuspecting fellow to jump several feet in the air. Purged from all further fantasies of Ardent Ample, the man raced away screaming.

"Return," yelled Mrs. Stetson. "Come back, you

poor sinner, and get yourself Rescued . . . before it's too late."

"Gee," said Soup, "this is fun. It's about as entertaining as watching Fearless Ferguson or Tex Ritter."

"And it's *free*," I said.

Soup shook his head. "Wrong, old sport. One of those ladies is holding a can with a slot in the top."

"What for?"

"Money," said Soup. "I got a hunch they're collecting profits for the Prophets."

"Be quiet," I warned Soup. "Mrs. Stetson's looking this way. If she sees that we're spying on her, she'll certain spill it all to our mothers."

Soup nodded.

"Right," he said.

Yet I noticed that, as he was watching Mrs. Stetson, Soup was smiling. I figured that his secret, whatever it was, had something to do with Mrs. Stetson, a wagon wheel and hay. In my mind, I couldn't quite assemble this weird combination of elements into any semblance of order. None of it made sense. Soup's ideas rarely did.

I looked up at the water tank. There it stood, a silent sentinel towering above the town of Learning; perhaps a warning to Soup and to me that we weren't allowed to go near it. Sheriff Dillon Blood had made his point as to the DANGER sign which we'd seen.

"Hey," said Soup, "somebody's coming out of the door of the theater."

It was Mr. Osgood Rivoli, the manager.

"I thought I just heard somebody scream," said Mr. Rivoli.

"You," snarled Mrs. Stetson. *"You're* the cause of the lion's share of *sin* in this town."

She shook her sign and another lady shook her can. Forward Mrs. Stetson charged, with her left and right flanks supported by the infantry advance of the other ladies. Mr. Rivoli's mouth opened, in panic. He was cornered and he knew it. Trapped like a rat.

"We're giving this town a *good cleansing,"* said Mrs. Stetson.

At first, I thought Mrs. Stetson was going to bash Mr. Rivoli over the head with her sign. But she resisted. What we saw next, however, was even more brutal than any beating.

Mrs. Stetson and the other women suddenly busted into their punishing anthem, "Rescued from the Burning Flames":

> Oh . . . how . . .
> Poker chips and scarlet lips were
> Darkening my life.
> Cigarettes, and race track bets I'd owe.
> Then I'd sight a shining light to
> Guide me from the strife.
> Rescued from the burning flames below.
>
> Fetch, fetch, fetch . . . this
> Poor and ragged wretch, from
> Sin and gin and all gin rummy games.

Vice isn't nice . . . it's
Worse than shooting dice.
Save me from those awful burning flames.

Oh . . . how . . .
Billiard balls and dancing halls were
Blackening my soul. I was
Even reading Edgar Allan Poe.
From despair, a golden stair would
Snatch me from The Hole.
Rescued from the burning flames below.

It sure was fun to watch.

As poor Mr. Rivoli was cowering in the corner, by
the movie theater's front door, he certain did appear
as though he wanted to be Rescued. But not from the
burning flames.

"You have to give Mrs. Stetson credit," Soup said.
"Her singing would make anybody pray."

Ten

"Rob," said Soup, "here we are."

It was Friday. The final day of school was over, and the two of us stood behind Wilbur's Wagon Repair.

"All we have to do now," said Soup, "is construct our stunt wagon for tomorrow's talent contest."

I stared at my pal. "*A wagon?*"

Soup nodded. "Sure. We have to find a container to hold all of our hay. And it's got to be something that rolls." Without further explanation, Soup pointed at a large wagon wheel. "That one there is good to start with. Bring it over here, like the good fellow you are."

I rolled it to Soup.

"We'll need three more," he said. But then he scratched his head. "What'll we use for a bin?"

"Search me," I told him. "I've never built a hay wagon before, and neither have you. Maybe we ought to ask Mr. Wilbur Wynfield if we can use this stuff."

"I already asked him," Soup said.

"He said *yes*?"

"No," said Soup, "he said *no*. But he hinted that maybe we could borrow some of the junk, as long as we bring it all back."

I sighed.

"Soup," I said, "if you ask me, I don't guess the two of us can build a wagon between now and chore time."

My pal made a face. "You're right, we probable can't. So best we do something else."

"Like what?"

Soup grinned. "We'll sort of borrow a junky wagon that's already built." He looked around the acre of debris. "There's bound to be one here somewhere. Rob, you search here, and I'll look over yonder, in that rubbish."

"Okay. But what if Mr. Wynfield comes out back and catches us?"

"He won't catch us."

"How come?"

"Because," said Soup, "I spotted him on his way to Miss Irma Crump's, carrying a saxophone."

I smiled.

What Soup was telling me seemed to fit into the overall spirit of the town. Almost everyone in Learning was preparing to display a talent to Hollywood Heartburn. But first they would be testing the instructional abilities of Miss Crump, perhaps stretching them to a breaking point. Or to early retirement.

Looking around, I pawed through mountain after mountain of junk, searching for some kind of a cart. Nothing completely assembled caught my eye. Soup's mention of hay and Mrs. Stetson kept looming in my mind. I felt suspicious of whatever it was that Soup was planning. Visions of Sheriff Dillon Blood kept creeping into my thoughts. Along with picturing myself in *jail*.

"Hey!"

It was Soup who had yelled.

"Rob," he hollered, "I found it."

Climbing over a heap of junk, I located Soup. There he was, standing on an object that looked very little like a hay wagon. In fact, it didn't look a whole lot like anything at all. The side of the contraption Soup had found bore lettering, old and faded. As my hand dusted it off, the letters emerged into view, spelling out how this strange vehicle had once been employed.

GIL'S GARBAGE.

One close-up whiff convinced me. Gil, whoever he was, perhaps had no longer been able to stand the stink, and had retired his wagon to rest in peace at Wilbur's. Or maybe Gil's horse had fainted from the aroma. The smell was so bad that it smarted my eyes. It reminded me of my own shirt.

I looked at Soup. "A garbage wagon?"

With a leap, Soup jumped lightly down.

"Hold on, Rob," he said. "This is no time to turn fussy. All we have to do is hose it off a mite. *Vision,* old sport! Don't see it as she is. Imagine what she'll become! Our ticket to Hollywood, fame and fortune." He paused, with a sly wink. "Not to mention the fact that you'll absolutely *wow* Norma Jean Bissell."

I thought about Norma Jean, a young lady who didn't smell at all like Gil's Garbage but of Bathsheba Bubble Bath. And, I was thinking, it was fortunate that the wagon smelled worse than I did.

Soup, meanwhile, had raced over to Mr. Wilbur Wynfield's shack, grabbed a hose, and was returning at a gallop, with a nozzle in hand. Water began to squirt a feeble and unenthusiastic stream.

Together, we hosed it down.

The fragrance of Gil's Garbage wagon didn't really improve. Somehow, the water seemed to freshen the scent, an aroma which would have gagged The Green Maggot.

"Yuk," I said. "It's getting worse."

"Nonsense," said Soup. "All we have to do is clip a clothespin on our noses. Then we won't smell it at all, because we'll also muffle the stink under the hay."

Up on the Gil's Garbage wagon he climbed, joyously jumping, waving both arms in the air.

I had to hand it to Soup.

Luther Wesley Vinson always seemed to thrive and flourish whenever the odds were pitted against us. His capacity for having fun overcame all of my most sensible suggestions. Soup's spirit, more contagious than chicken pox, abounded. Seeing his smile, I had to admit how lucky I was to have Soup for a pal.

Yet the wagon was neither large nor impressive. It just slumped among the litter as if it had somehow found a place to hide, as though ashamed.

"Don't look at this thing as it is, Rob," he said, cracking a wider grin. "See it as it'll be tomorrow . . . our golden chariot to Hollywood. I bet we'll even amaze Mrs. Stetson."

There he stood, atop Gil's Garbage wagon, waving his arms and smiling with neither a care nor a caution. I had to give him credit. Soup Vinson, garbage or no garbage, wouldn't be denied any of the laurels of life. His happiness at finding our wagon, sloppy though it was, had converted him into Santa Claus, a circus clown and the Easter bunny.

"Wow," he said. "This is it."

"It sure is," I said, holding my nose.

"Rob, just wait until Fearless Ferguson sees what we're going to do. He'll beg us to be stars in his next movie."

"Exactly what *are* we doing?"

"A stunt," Soup told me.

"A stunt with Gil's Garbage?"

Again he leaped to the ground. "Yes, old sport. A

stunt that will probable electrify all the people in town. We'll dazzle them with our daring. You and I shall be the talk of Learning. Heroes to young and old. Fearless will be standing silently bug-eyed as Rob Peck and Soup Vinson, amid the cheering and confetti, come rolling to a glittering glory. Fearless Ferguson will be holding his breath in awe."

"How?" I asked, realizing that all the people in town would be holding their breaths to avoid a whiff of Gil's Garbage.

"It's going to be a surprise," said Soup. "Because if you know about it now, it could dull the impact of tomorrow's triumph."

Suddenly I smelled more than garbage. I smelled trouble. It was another Luther Wesley Vinson blueprint for some horrible wagon ride, with hay, inspired by none other than Mrs. Stetson.

How, I again wondered, would all of Soup's crazy parts fit together into our winning the talent show? As I recalled, Soup had mentioned Dugan's Hill and gravity, along with Bishop Zion Zeal's anthem about sin.

"I don't like it, Soup," I said.

"It'll work."

"You mean we'll be riding into town as two lumps of Gil's Garbage?"

"Not quite." Soup rested a soiled hand on my shoulder. "Rob, old sport, just trust me. I'm the guy who's never let you down."

Secretly, I had to admit that Soup Vinson was right.

Somehow, blessed with luck, his ideas usual brought us out of a mess. The trouble was, it was always Soup who had created the mess in the first place. And if Gil's Garbage wagon wasn't already about as messy as possible, Soup would nudge it closer to an unhappy ending.

Yet, perhaps there was a brighter side.

According to Soup, we were about to blend Gil's Garbage with Mrs. Stetson. Inwardly, I laughed. Maybe it would be just the trick to unite our town, instead of dividing it. For sure, we had good citizens in both camps, the Talent Show people as well as the Golden Prophets.

But, I wondered, could Soup and I really pull it off? Would we keep everybody friendly on Saturday? It seemed more important than winning a talent show.

Still holding my nose, I stared at the garbage wagon. Nobody in his right mind, I was deciding, would link it with any semblance of talent. But then Soup was rarely in his right mind. Possibly it was my duty to point out the difference between talent and trash.

Soup, once again, removed the strange paper from his pocket, unfolded it, and pretended to decipher its mystery.

"Is that your map?" I asked him.

"Yup. Because without a map, old top, we don't have a route to victory. Our success may depend on geography as well as timing."

"Okay," I said, my palms sweating. "As long as we keep clear of jail."

Soup frowned. "There's something missing," he said. "We need *one* more thing. Or"—he began a slow smile—"maybe *two.*"

"What are they?"

"Well," said Soup, "just last evening, my mother commented that Miss Edith Terwilliger is coming tomorrow."

"Who's she?"

"She's my mother's cousin. Slightly nuts, and lives up north in Thurgood. She'll be entering her animals in the talent show. So I bet she wouldn't care if we briefly borrowed the use of Bulgar and Vulgar, to pull our little wagon."

"Bulgar . . . and Vulgar? Are they horses?"

Soup grinned. "Almost."

Eleven

Saturday finally came.

So did everyone and everything. As Soup and I stood on Main Street, I'd never seen so many people, animals, musical instruments, costumes and out-of-town visitors.

"Look," said Soup, "here comes Lem in his cowboy suit and leading Romeo by the nose."

Mr. Lem Seegood was well known in town, *not* as a cowboy who rode a horse, but rather as a fellow who was always trying to ride a bull. Romeo, in tow, looked bigger and meaner than ever, and certainly not in the mood to be ridden.

Lem stopped to chat with Mrs. Emma Fulsome

and her parrot, Captain Kidd, who could recite the opening lines of a poem, "If," by Rudyard Kipling.

"Hey," I said to Soup, "there's Fred."

According to local gossip, Mr. Fred Muller's unique talent was his ability to play "Flight of the Bumble Bee" on a cigar-box violin, while totally covered by his swarm of honeybees.

He nodded to Miss Grace A. Mason, a local spinster, who was practicing her act, playing an ocarina with her nose while clog-dancing in ski boots. To make her feat even more difficult, each boot was attached to a ski. Some people referred to her as A. Mason Grace.

Nearby, a husband and wife were busily occupied with a ten-foot vertical xylophone, silvery in color, the gaseous tones of which were produced by rapidly working a tire pump. Selma and Orrin Minotti called it their Musical Zipper, which is what it looked like.

"Keep pumping, Selma," shouted Orrin to his perspiring wife, "so I can practice 'Nola.'"

"Where's your mother's cousin?" I asked Soup.

"We'll find her," Soup announced. "We can't miss spotting a team like Bulgar and Vulgar. Let's go look."

Rounding a corner, we saw a small crowd of people listening blank-faced to a very large man, dressed in a shiny crimson robe, preaching atop a high freight box.

"That's got to be Bishop Zion Zeal," said Soup.

"How can you tell?" I asked him.

"Because so many of his Golden Prophets of Eternal Glory are passing collection plates. Looks like the Prophets are raking in the golden profits."

As Bishop Zeal's sermon finally paused for a momentary breather (as well as a fiscal accounting), the Golden Prophet choir, in gold robes, began to sing "Rescued from the Burning Flames." Nearby, I saw Mrs. Stetson, waving her sign on a stick, keeping time to the anthem. Her sign read "GIN IS SIN."

Other nonsinging Prophets, robed in green and blue, passed out pamphlets and accosted bystanders by inquiring, "Have you been Rescued?" One farmer responded by saying that he hadn't even been inoculated, and Mrs. Stetson tried to whack him with her sign.

"Let's get out of here," Soup said quickly, "before Mrs. Stetson gets us Rescued for the entire day."

We ran.

But we stopped to listen, for as long as we could bear it, to Mr. Elbert Higgin, who was practicing on his giant tarnished sousaphone. I wasn't quite sure, but I think he was attempting to play "Beautiful Dreamer." His solo was accompanied by his cow, Cleopatra, who could wag her tail high in the air somewhat like an orchestra leader's wand.

We heard cheering.

Sure enough, a shiny black limousine had pulled into town, and out hopped the famous radio personality himself, Mr. Hollywood Heartburn. There he stood, handsome, tan, tall and smiling. A lady rushed up for an autograph and Hollywood cheerfully obliged. The rewarded fan waved the signature for her jealous friends to behold.

Soup and I both were jumping up and down, trying to see over the grown-up heads in front of us. To no avail, so we ducked down and scurried like spooked rodents between legs and feet, until we were really up close to the big black car.

Lettered on its flank in glittering silver were the famous words.

HOLLYWOOD HEARTBURN'S TALENT SHOW

"Wow," said Soup, "he's really here."

"He sure is," I said.

"But I wonder," said Soup, "when we're going to meet Fearless Ferguson."

I heard a fancy car horn sound.

Pulling up behind Hollywood Heartburn's black limousine came another car, as large and as long, and whiter than a Monday night bedsheet. Hollywood Heartburn turned to wave at the white car.

"Folks," he said generously, "here comes the Hollywood star y'all truly are here to meet in person. So let's give a big welcome cheer for . . . Fearless Ferguson!"

I held my breath.

But, for some reason, no door of the big white car opened. People crushed around close to sneak a peek inside.

"Fans," said Hollywood Heartburn, "you'll have to be somewhat indulgent with Fearless. Because there's only one thing in the whole entire world that frightens him."

"What's that?" Soup asked him.

Hollywood shrugged.

"People," he said. "As long as I've known Mr. Fearless Ferguson, he's always been rather *shy* whenever he has to face a crowd. In fact, sometimes he runs away to *hide.*"

"I want his autograph," said Soup.

"Yeah, me too," I added.

Smiling down at us, Mr. Hollywood Heartburn rested a sparkle-ringed hand on each of our shoulders.

"Boys," he said, "you'll get your chance to shake hands with Fearless. But maybe not right away. He'll have to emerge from his car in his own sweet time. He just needs a few minutes to adjust to a new environment."

I looked around, yet I certain didn't see an environment, whatever that was.

"However," said Hollywood, raising his hands and talking confidently to the crowd, "we've got a bigger surprise in store for you people." He pointed along Main Street to an approaching vehicle, a *truck,* big enough to be a house. A construction truck. Never had I seen a dump truck so gigantic. It also had a very loud horn. With my eyes wide open, I saw the truck stop. Its bin was piled high with a mysterious cargo, a pink powdery substance.

"What is it?" somebody asked.

Hollywood Heartburn's face flashed a benevolent grin. "That," he said proudly, "is our gift to the town. Absolutely *free*! It's a truckful of . . . Bathsheba Bubble Bath."

Right on cue, the truck's bin began to tilt, and a huge pile of pink powder was dumped on Main Street. As far as I knew, it was even higher than Andy's Mountain.

As the enormous dump truck lowered its bin, then rolled away, every lady in town, plus dozens of little girls, all screamed in unison, their faces ecstatic with joy. One grateful matron after another rushed forward to present a hug to Mr. Hollywood Heartburn.

"Aw," he said modestly, "don't thank me, ladies. Actually it was my sponsor's idea. But I wasn't kidding about its being a gift. Soon as the talent show is over, all of you ladies can help yourselves to as much strawberry-scented Bathsheba Bubble Bath as you can carry home. That ought to amount to about a year's supply for every family in the entire county."

The ladies were squealing with anticipation.

"And it's all *free*!"

They squealed louder.

As I watched the entire female population of Learning milling around the mountain of pink powder, I was wondering if Norma Jean Bissell was there too. I couldn't spot her. The crowd was too large.

The radio star raised his hands.

"And now," said Hollywood Heartburn, "it's about time we started to judge all the local talent. Who knows," he almost whispered, "there may be a motion picture audition awaiting somebody in this town. And that'll mean an all-expenses-paid trip to . . . Hollywood!"

People shrieked.

Women screamed and strong men fainted. *Hollywood,* like *free,* was a magic word. As far as the tiny town of Learning, Vermont, was concerned, a place such as Hollywood, California, was equidistant from our community as Saturn.

We knew about Hollywood.

The Depression, a current period of hard times, had forced many a local resident to tighten his belt. Yet the patronage at State Theater continued to thrive. It was our only extravagance, a quarter's worth (a dime for kids) of escape to black-and-white celluloid nightclubs, where Ginger Rogers and Fred Astaire tapped on white pianos. Or to see Fearless Ferguson halt a runaway stagecoach carrying a cargo of Sunday-picnic-bound orphans.

But abruptly the reverie of the moment was clouded by the unexpected appearance of Mrs. Stetson, supported by an entourage of Golden Prophets of Eternal Glory as well as Bishop Zeal.

Mrs. Stetson was toting a freshly painted placard, which firmly stated its message.

BUBBLE BATH
MEANS
HEAVEN'S WRATH

The overwhelming majority of the ladies of Learning, however, were not to be denied their share of pink loot. It wasn't every day that Bathsheba Bubble Bath was given away for nothing, and even the more ardent churchgoers were anxious to claim their cut of a pinker life, the irresistible pleasure that the most glamorous Hollywood stars dump in their private bathtubs.

Somehow, order was restored, and the talent contest swung into high gear.

Even though the Golden Prophets of Eternal Glory blasted out "Rescued from the Burning Flames," the talented and untalented presented their artistry to the suffering ears and eyes of Hollywood Heartburn and his crew of judges.

The Musical Zipper performed first.

Selma Minotti pumped her pump while Orrin bleated out what almost passed for melody on their impressive invention, the vertical xylophone. But suddenly their rendition of "Nola" gasped to a halt.

"Oh, no," wailed Orrin.

"What's the matter?" asked his sweating and pumping partner.

"Darn," said Orrin, "my Zipper's stuck."

Twelve

The afternoon wore on.

"Well," said Soup, "it's about time."

"Okay," I said, wondering what it was that my pal, Soup Vinson, was intending to do next.

"Rob, if you'll trot up Dugan's Hill and start loading that hay into the wagon, I'll find my mother's cousin. Then I'll meet you behind Wilbur's Wagon Repair."

"I don't want to load all of Janice's hay by myself," I told him.

"You won't have to," Soup said. "I'll lend you a helping hand with the hay, as soon as I arrive with Bulgar and Vulgar."

"Our *almost horses*," I said.

Soup winked. "Right. So get going. I'll join you up on the hill in about ten minutes. You'll see me coming and I'll probable need assistance."

Turning, I huffed up Dugan's Hill, wondering what Soup was really up to, but mostly about Bulgar and Vulgar. Out of breath from my uphill scamper, I panted to a stop behind Wilbur's Wagon Repair. Looking around the acre of clutter I couldn't quite remember where Soup and I had our hay hidden.

To be more honest, Janice's hay.

But then I found it, yanked away the old tarpaulin and began loading the hay into Gil's Garbage wagon. Load after load I lugged, until every wispy straw had been moved. None of it made sense.

"Rob!"

It was Soup who had hollered my name. As I twisted my head, I saw him being dragged by two enormous black-and-white spotted animals. At first they looked like Holstein cows. Yet as they approached, I imagined that they were closer in size to killer whales.

One of them barked.

I didn't know whether it was Bulgar or Vulgar, and I didn't care, because I was too scared. The two gigantic dogs were heading my way. Soup was behind, being dragged through the dirt on his belly, yet clinging to their long leather leashes.

"Help me," Soup yelled with a mouthful of dirt. "Grab one of them. I can't hold tight much longer."

Why I did it, I'll never understand, but I managed to grab a leash just as Soup let go.

Before today, I'd been to a lot of places, and to many of them in a hurry. Yet never before had I been dragged through piles of trash by a dog that thought he was a racing car. Soup was being dragged too.

"Hang on," he yelled to me. "They're getting tired."

"*They're* getting tired," I said, as my face plowed through another obstacle of debris. "What about *us*?"

Finally, the dogs loped to a stop, stilled, and licked our dirty faces. As I stood up, my dog was taller than I was.

"Is this Bulgar or Vulgar?" I asked Soup.

Soup lay on the ground, holding a leash and panting. "Who cares?" he said. But then his customary exuberance returned, and he rose slowly to his feet and grinned. "Come on, Rob. Let's go hitch these animals to Gil's Garbage and win the talent show."

"What kind of dogs are they?" I asked.

Soup smiled. "Siberian bearhounds."

"They look more like Siberian bears."

I patted Bulgar, or maybe it was Vulgar, as I spat out a mouthful of Vermont topsoil.

"Rob, old sport, it all fits my plan. All we have to do now is hitch Bulgar and Vulgar to the two front corners of our garbage wagon, and into town we fly."

"Suppose they don't want to go?"

Both dogs were wagging their tails. One of the tails hit my head, and it felt somewhat like being struck by Babe Ruth's baseball bat. It knocked me to the ground.

"See," said Soup, "how friendly they are."

As I got up, Bulgar (or Vulgar) bent down to lick my cheek again.

"He's telling you he's sorry," Soup said.

I rubbed the welt on the back of my neck. "Soup, are you certain these animals are *dogs*?"

"Not really," Soup told me. "My mother's cousin, Miss Terwilliger, said they're still . . . puppies."

I looked up at the dog's face.

"Puppies?"

"That's what she told me."

"What'll they be when they're final grown? They won't be dogs. They'll be a couple of hairy mammoths . . . with tusks."

Soup laughed.

"Come on," he said, "and let's coax these monsters to our wagon. If we can. Then make our grand entrance into town, and amaze everybody. And you'll surely catch the eye of Norma Jean Bissell."

That did it.

We headed, more or less, around the main building of Wilbur's Wagon Repair in order to locate our little cart.

Luckily for us, our team of elephants who thought they were dogs led the way, and willingly. Bulgar and Vulgar seemed to be in tune with the general spirit of a Saturday talent show. But we still held tight to their leashes.

We came to our wagon.

"I had to load all the hay myself," I told Soup, "without your help."

"Next time," Soup told me, "I'll load the hay, and *you* can be in charge of Bulgar and Vulgar."

"No thanks."

Gil's Garbage wagon still smelled of its long-ago cargo. Despite the hosing, the stench was almost unbearable.

"Did you bring a clothespin?" Soup asked, pulling one from his pocket.

"I sure did," I said.

Soup pinched his nose with a clothespin, which I did likewise for mine. Yet I could still smell the unpleasant fumes. Somehow, they seemed to be invading my pores, finding my nose and then tormenting it. I even noticed that Bulgar and Vulgar helped themselves to only one brief sniff of our vehicle.

"Okay," said Soup, "all we do now is hitch these two monsters to the front and then merrily roll along to fame and fortune."

There was no doubt in my mind about Bulgar's and Vulgar's muscular capacities. For what little I'd seen and felt, these two Siberian bearhounds could have pulled Siberia.

"Hurry," said Soup, "or we'll miss out on all the talent judging." As he knotted the end of a leash to a front corner of our wagon, he was grinning. "I'll just bet that nobody else thinks of entering the contest as stuntmen."

"You're probable right," I snorted through my clothespin. "Everyone else has either talent or common sense."

"Rob, is your dog hitched?"

"Sort of."

"Okay, climb aboard."

Soup was already up on the rotten old wagon seat, and I joined him. In Soup's hand was a long willow switch.

"What's that for?" I asked.

"To make Bulgar and Vulgar run faster."

"But," I said, "it's all downhill."

"All the better," said Soup. "We'll be able to make a more exciting spectacle the faster we go." He looked around. "I wonder what could be keeping Janice."

I almost choked. "Janice Riker?"

Soup grinned. "Yeah. I told her about our borrowing a lot of her goat hay."

My mouth popped open. "You *told* her?"

"Right." Soup winked. "And if I know Janice, she'll be really steaming about now. In fact, I'd guess she's mad enough to do something about it. Something mean. And *we* won't have to shoulder all of the *blame*."

"Soup," I said, "you're really nuts."

As I looked around in furtive terror, I spotted Janice rumbling our way. She was dressed as Shirley Dimple; a frilly dress, long white stockings and wearing a blond wig. Yet I sure knew who it was as she rounded the corner of Wilbur's shop. Janice held something in her hand which looked like a small box. I prayed it wasn't dynamite.

"Hurry," I told Soup. "She's coming!"

Soup prodded Bulgar and Vulgar into a slow trot, yet Janice was coming up behind us and gaining.

"Faster," I said to Soup.

"She's *supposed* to catch us, Rob. It's all part of my scheme. If you think about Mrs. Stetson, you'll understand, then bow to my cunning. In fact, I even begged Janice not to bring what I'm hoping she brought."

Sure enough, Janice caught us. Still running, she pulled a match from the box she was carrying, lit it and tossed it into the hay. Then threw in another and another.

"Gotcha," said Janice, baring her fangs.

As our load of hay ignited, Soup, using his switch, whacked Bulgar and Vulgar into a gallop. Soup, I was thinking, had gone crazy again. Now we were on fire. Hay aflame, Gil's Garbage wagon lurched forward, and we were heading down Dugan's Hill toward town, yanked forward by two of the world's most enthusiastic animals.

"Help!"

I heard a strange voice. It wasn't Soup's. The single word came from behind us. Somebody was hiding under the hay. As I turned around, a head popped up in front of where the hay was burning. And I saw a face I knew as well as I knew my own or Soup's.

It was Fearless Ferguson!

But he wasn't looking very fearless. His face was nothing except sheer panic. "I was hiding," he said. "Because I'm afraid to meet people in person. Where are we going?"

"Down Dugan's Hill," said Soup.

Meanwhile, our two Siberian bearhounds, Bulgar and Vulgar, had somehow decided that pulling Gil's Garbage wagon was fun. They bolted downward as though shot out of a cannon.

"Hang on," Soup was yelling. "Yahoo!"

Down the hill raced our burning wagon, faster and faster, heading toward Main Street and also hopefully to fortune, fame and a promising career as movie stuntmen. Having old Fearless Ferguson along would, I was thinking, serve to brighten our image.

"We're going too fast," wailed Fearless. "And I think the wagon's burning too."

Ahead, I saw another problem.

Romeo, the romantic bull, was chasing Cleopatra, the musical cow. Perhaps with a duet in mind. But as Cleopatra trotted across our path, pursued by a highly interested bull, Bulgar and Vulgar varied our route.

Instead of rolling straight down the hill toward Main Street, as Soup's map had originally outlined, Gil's Garbage wagon was now bouncing along, with neither steering wheel nor rudder, intent upon a collision. The warning words of Sheriff Dillon Blood echoed in my frantic mind.

"Turn," Soup ordered the dogs.

Miraculously, they turned. In opposite directions, one to the left and the other to the right. As both of their leashes snapped, Bulgar and Vulgar raced off after Romeo and Cleopatra, free and clear, knocking over the hive which held Fred Muller's bees.

Our wagon, now a dogless runaway, seemed to possess an evil mind of its own. And dead ahead stood its intended target.

The water tower!

Thirteen

"No," whispered Soup.

"Let's jump off," I said.

"But we're going too fast."

Behind me, I could hear the crackle of burning hay plus a few scraps of cooking garbage. Not to mention an increasingly warm Mr. Ferguson, who had crawled forward to join us.

Soup and I gripped the wagon seat, as Fearless Ferguson hid behind it. We were halfway down Dugan's Hill at a place where the grade was steepest. Gil's Garbage wagon was practically flying. Worse yet, our speed was fanning the flames.

We hit a big bump!

"Hey," said Soup. "If we lean, we'll miss the water tower and coast to a stop up the pile of bath powder."

We leaned.

Somewhere, below us in town, the Golden Prophet choir was singing their anthem, "Rescued from the Burning Flames."

It didn't do any good.

Fearless Ferguson screamed and pointed dead ahead.

As our smoking wagon picked up speed, I could see that we were bound to crash. Luckily, only one leg of the water tower seemed to be our target. Closer and closer we raced, so close that I could see the warning sign near the ladder and even read its red letters.

DANGER

"Don't worry, Mr. Ferguson," said Soup. "Nobody in town will ever guess that *you're* scared."

"Nobody," wailed Fearless, "except the laundry."

Ahead, the nearest leg of the water tower lay only thirty feet away. Twenty feet. Ten. Five. One. . . . Closing my eyes, I grabbed the wagon seat and Fearless Ferguson, preparing to die. If I died, at least I wouldn't have to go to jail.

CRACK!

We didn't quite crash.

Instead, the front corner of Gil's Garbage wagon glanced against the rotten tower leg, and several things happened in the next five seconds. A wheel came off. Boards flew loose. People saw us and screeched in panic. Burning hay filled the air. But, believable or not, our wagon actually headed according to Soup's prediction . . . straight toward the big soft truckload of pink powder.

Even though, in the past, I'd tried many times to do a front triple flip off a diving board into Putt's Pond, my flip was always a flop. This time, however, as Gil's Garbage wagon (or whatever was left of it) dived headlong into the soft pile . . . POOF . . . my world turned upside down at least three times.

I landed in powder, feet first.

"Wow," said Soup. "I feel like a jigsaw puzzle that's missing half its pieces."

The two of us were about waist-deep in bath powder, legs down. But poor Mr. Ferguson was also waist-deep, legs up. Grabbing his ankles, we extracted him, then brushed the pink powder from his face and hair.

"Gee," I said, "we saved Fearless Ferguson!"

Looking around for Norma Jean, I realized that I now smelled worse than usual, thanks to my wild ride aboard Gil's Garbage cart. And I was hoping that Norma Jean Bissell's nose would happen to be wearing a clothespin.

"I stink," I confessed. "I really stink."

Nearby, the escaped bees seemed to be even more upset and were swarming everywhere, perhaps excited by the smell of garbage. One particular bee stung a Golden Prophet, and I heard him mention God.

"But," said Soup, "we're finally safe. Our smoke will drive away the bees."

He removed the clothespin from his nose, and I did likewise. And my pal was right. I could smell smoke aplenty.

"Hey," I said quickly, "I think this mountain of pink bath powder is on *fire*."

It was!

Every female voice in town was now wailing. Not over their fear of fire, or bees, but because the mountain of *free* Bathsheba Bubble Bath would burn.

Golden Prophets, however, were happily beaming, predicting that all the evil bubble bath powder would justly be consumed in flame. Harsh words were being exchanged. Faces frowned. People didn't seem to be friendly anymore.

"Water," demanded Bishop Zion Zeal, as he pointed at the local ladies, who were on the verge of tears. "Bring me water, to baptize these wretched sinners and Rescue them from the burning flames. I'll *cleanse* this town forever. *Bring me water!*"

I heard a fire siren.

Good news. The Learning Volunteer Fire Department, commanded by Chief Thermal Keyo, was on its way, armed with a hose.

"Saved again," said Soup.

But then I heard another voice of alarm, this time in total panic. "Look out!" the voice of Sheriff Blood was warning.

As I looked, I saw it happen. The one horrible catastrophe that Learning never thought could possibly occur . . . one to fulfill Bishop Zeal's fervent request.

The rotten leg of the water tower cracked, bent, then buckled. High in the air, the giant tank of water began to sway and tremble. As the tower leg gave way, the huge water tank started to tip, totter and fall.

"Run!" somebody shouted. "Run for your lives!"

Down tumbled the water tank, landing very nearby. As the large iron-banded tub shattered into splinters, the tons and tons of water sloshed toward us. We were caught like rats in a flood.

My feet were still stuck in the powder.

Unable to run, I just stood with Soup and Fearless Ferguson on top of the pink mountain. Wide-eyed, I saw the tidal wave approaching. And it came. As it reached us, I heard a mighty HISSSSS, as an ocean of water united with tons of Bathsheba Bubble Bath.

Suddenly we were no longer a town. Learning had become an enormous cloud of expanding bubbles enriched with K-34.

Foam was spreading everywhere.

Nothing except strawberry-scented bubbles. I couldn't even see Soup or Fearless Ferguson, but I could swear I heard Mrs. Stetson, in panic, shout a forbidden term. Bulgar and Vulgar were joyously barking, and Mrs. Emma Fulsome's pet parrot, Captain Kidd, said a word too. And it sure wasn't *If*.

Bubbles. Foam. Fragrance. Ours was a pink Bathsheba world. A strawberry meringue pie.

"Rob," I heard Soup yelling, "where are ya?"

"Over here," I answered, "buried in bubbles."

"Thank goodness," said Fearless Ferguson, "I finally have a place to hide that isn't on fire."

Off to my right came a contented bovine sigh, which sounded as though Romeo had finally caught up to Cleopatra. Then I heard voices which I recognized as those belonging to Mr. and Mrs. Riker.

"Keep tap-dancing, Janice. You'll win."

I still couldn't see anyone, being totally engulfed in Bathsheba Bubble Bath. I'd never smelled more fragrant as I fought to survive amid my luxurious soaking in a galaxy of pink pearls.

One by one, however, a trillion pink bubbles of Bathsheba began to pop, and the town of Learning and its pore-emulsified citizens started to reappear, all of them frosted with froth.

I was still neck-deep in Bathsheba Bubble Bath and so was Soup. But as we looked at each other, neither of us seemed to care. Nor did anyone else, possibly with the exception of Mrs. Stetson, Bishop Zion Zeal and the Golden Prophets of Eternal Glory.

Smiles, however, began to adorn even their stern faces as well, as people everywhere were joining in song, "Rescued from the Burning Flames."

It could hardly have been described as music, because so many of Miss Irma Crump's underrehearsed instrumentalists were attempting to convert the anthem into a mass recital.

"Amen," said Mrs. Stetson. "The town is *cleansed* by a *miracle.*"

I felt a large hand on my shoulder. Turning, I looked up and saw a suds-covered Sheriff Dillon Blood.

"Are we going to jail?" I asked him.

He smiled, bubbles and all. "No," he said. "I'm glad your smoke saved everybody from those pesky bees." He patted us on the back. "And I'm plain grateful that our water tower problem finally got took care of, without nobody getting hurt." He smiled again. "Most important, you two lads have united the entire town. See for yourself."

I saw.

Mrs. Stetson was shaking hands with Fearless Ferguson. Nearby, shoulder to shoulder and singing, stood Bishop Zion Zeal and Hollywood Heartburn. The parrot was singing too, somewhat better than Mrs. Stetson.

Soup was busy hauling an exhausted Bulgar and Vulgar back to their owner, his mother's cousin, Miss Terwilliger. So I had a spare moment to look around for Norma Jean Bissell and spotted her. Seeing as both of us were still up to our knees in the rapidly diminishing soap bubbles, I sloshed casually in her general direction. Hooking thumbs into my belt, I dazzled her with conversational sparkle.

"Hi," I said. "Smell me."

"I already have," she said. "Yesterday in school.

You're nice, but *you* and *washing* are total strangers."

I drew an inch closer. "Smell me now," I said, exuding the social confidence which only K-34 could provide.

"You smell very sweet," said Norma Jean. "You ought to make Bathsheba Bubble Bath a regular habit."

"I plan to." I grinned. "Every spring."

Robert Newton Peck is the author of forty-one books. *Soup on Fire* is the ninth adventure about Soup and Rob, who also star in Peck's ABC-TV Specials. Mr. Peck won the 1982 Mark Twain award, and often visits schools, colleges, and writers conferences to lecture on writing and to play ragtime piano.

Young readers who wish to write to Robert Newton Peck should be informed that letters that get quick answers are those with a school address, and not a home address.

> Robert Newton Peck
> 500 Sweetwater Club Circle
> Longwood, FL 32779

Robert Newton Peck and his friend, Sunday